Lord, Teach Us To Pray

Andrew Murray

About the Author

Andrew Murray

Andrew Murray (9 May 1828 – 18 January 1917) was a South African writer, teacher and Christian pastor. Murray considered missions to be "the chief end of the church". Andrew Murray was the second child of Andrew Murray Sr. (1794–1866), a Dutch Reformed Church missionary sent from Scotland to South Africa. He was born in Graaff Reinet, South Africa. His mother, Maria Susanna Stegmann, was of French Huguenot and German Lutheran descent.

Murray was sent to Aberdeen in Scotland for his initial education, together with his elder brother, John. Both remained there until they obtained their master's degrees in 1845. From there, they both went to the University of Utrecht where they studied theology. The two brothers became members of Het Réveil, a religious revival movement opposed to the rationalism which was in vogue in the Netherlands at that time. Both brothers were ordained by the Hague Committee of the Dutch Reformed Church on 9 May 1848 and returned to the Cape.

Murray married Emma Rutherford in Cape Town, South Africa, on 2 July 1856. They had eight children together (four boys and four girls).

THE ONLY TEACHER

The disciples had been with Christ, and seen Him pray. They had learnt to understand something of the connection between His wondrous life in public, and His secret life of prayer. They had learnt to believe in Him as a Master in the art of prayer—none could pray like Him. And so they came to Him with the request, 'Lord, teach us to pray.' And in after years they would have told us that there were few things more wonderful or blessed that He taught them than His lessons on prayer.

And now still it comes to pass, as He is praying in a certain place, that disciples who see Him thus engaged feel the need of repeating the same request, 'Lord, teach us to pray.' As we grow in the [6]Christian life, the thought and the faith of the Beloved Master in His never-failing intercession becomes evermore precious, and the hope of being Like Christ in His intercession gains an attractiveness before unknown. And as we see Him pray, and remember that there is none who can pray like Him, and none who can teach like Him, we feel the petition of the disciples, 'Lord, teach us to pray,' is just what we need. And as we think how all He is and has, how He Himself is our very own, how He is Himself our life, we feel assured that we have but to ask, and He will be delighted to take us up into closer fellowship with Himself, and teach us to pray even as He prays.

Come, my brothers! Shall we not go to the Blessed Master and ask Him to enrol our names too anew in that school which He always keeps open for those who long to continue their studies in the Divine art of prayer and intercession? Yes, let us this very day say to the Master, as they did of old, 'Lord, teach us to pray.' As we meditate we shall find each word of the petition we bring to be full of meaning.

'Lord, teach us to pray.' Yes, to pray. This is what we need to be taught. Though in its beginnings prayer is so simple that the feeble child can pray, yet it is at the same time the highest and holiest work to which man can rise. It is fellowship with the Unseen and Most Holy One. The powers [7]of the eternal world have been placed at its disposal. It is the very essence of true religion, the channel of all blessings, the secret of power and life. Not only for ourselves, but for others, for the Church, for the world, it is to prayer that God has given the right to take hold of Him and His strength. It is on prayer that the promises wait for their fulfilment, the kingdom for its coming, the glory of God for its full revelation. And for this blessed work, how slothful and unfit we are. It is only the Spirit of God can enable us to do it aright. How speedily we are deceived into a resting in the form, while the power is wanting. Our early training, the teaching of the Church, the influence of habit, the stirring of the emotions—how easily these lead to prayer which has no spiritual power, and avails but little. True prayer, that takes hold of God's strength, that availeth much, to which the gates of heaven are really opened wide—who would not cry, Oh for some one to teach me thus to pray?

Jesus has opened a school, in which He trains His redeemed ones, who specially desire it, to have power in prayer. Shall we not enter it with the petition, Lord! it is just this we need to be taught! O teach us to pray.

'Lord, teach us to pray.' Yes, us, Lord. We have read in Thy Word with what power Thy believing people of old used to pray, and what mighty [8]wonders were done in answer to their prayers. And if this took place under the Old Covenant, in the time of preparation, how much more wilt Thou not now, in these days of fulfilment, give Thy people this sure sign of Thy presence in their midst. We have heard the promises given to Thine apostles of the power of prayer in Thy name, and have seen how gloriously they experienced their truth: we know for certain, they can become true to us too. We hear continually even in these days what glorious tokens of Thy power Thou dost still give to those who trust Thee fully. Lord! these all are men of like passions with ourselves; teach us to pray so too. The promises are for us, the powers and gifts of the heavenly world are for us. O teach us to pray so that we may receive abundantly. To us too Thou hast entrusted Thy work, on our prayer too the coming of Thy kingdom depends, in our prayer too Thou canst glorify Thy name; 'Lord, teach us to pray.' Yes, us,

6

Lord; we offer ourselves as learners; we would indeed be taught of Thee. 'Lord, teach us to pray.'

'Lord, teach us to pray.' Yes, we feel the need now of being taught to pray. At first there is no work appears so simple; later on, none that is more difficult; and the confession is forced from us: We know not how to pray as we ought. It is true we have God's Word, with its clear and sure promises; but sin has so darkened our mind, that we know not [9]always how to apply the Word. In spiritual things we do not always seek the most needful things, or fail in praying according to the law of the sanctuary. In temporal things we are still less able to avail ourselves of the wonderful liberty our Father has given us to ask what we need. And even when we know what to ask, how much there is still needed to make prayer acceptable. It must be to the glory of God, in full surrender to His will, in full assurance of faith, in the name of Jesus, and with a perseverance that, if need be, refuses to be denied. All this must be learned. It can only be learned in the school of much prayer, for practice makes perfect. Amid the painful consciousness of ignorance and unworthiness, in the struggle between believing and doubting, the heavenly art of effectual prayer is learnt. Because, even when we do not remember it, there is One, the Beginner and Finisher of faith and prayer, who watches over our praying, and sees to it that in all who trust Him for it their education in the school of prayer shall be carried on to perfection. Let but the deep undertone of all our prayer be the teachableness that comes from a sense of ignorance, and from faith in Him as a perfect teacher, and we may be sure we shall be taught, we shall learn to pray in power. Yes, we may depend upon it, He teaches to pray.

'Lord, teach us to pray.' None can teach like Jesus, none but Jesus; therefore we call on Him, [10]'Lord, teach us to pray.' A pupil needs a teacher, who knows his work, who has the gift of teaching, who in patience and love will descend to the pupil's needs. Blessed be God! Jesus is all this and much more. He knows what prayer is. It is Jesus, praying Himself, who teaches to pray. He knows what prayer is. He learned it amid the trials and tears of His earthly life. In heaven it is still His beloved work: His life there is prayer. Nothing delights Him more than to find those whom He can take with Him into the Father's presence, whom He can clothe with power to pray down God's blessing on those around them, whom He can train to be His fellow-workers in the intercession by which the kingdom is to be revealed on earth. He knows how to teach. Now by the urgency of felt need, then by the confidence with which joy inspires. Here by the teaching of the Word, there by the testimony of another believer who knows what it is to have prayer heard. By His Holy Spirit, He has access to our heart, and teaches us to pray by showing us the sin that hinders the prayer, or giving us the assurance that we please God. He teaches, by giving not only thoughts of what to ask or how to ask, but by breathing within us the very spirit of prayer, by living within us as the Great Intercessor. We may indeed and most joyfully say, 'Who teacheth like Him?' Jesus never taught His disciples how to preach, only how to pray. He [11]did not speak much of what was needed to preach well, but much of praying well. To know how to speak to God is more than knowing how to speak to man. Not power with men, but power with God is the first thing. Jesus loves to teach us how to pray.

What think you, my beloved fellow-disciples! would it not be just what we need, to ask the Master for a month to give us a course of special lessons on the art of prayer? As we meditate on the words He spake on earth, let us yield ourselves to His teaching in the fullest confidence that, with such a teacher, we shall make progress. Let us take time not only to meditate, but to pray, to tarry at the foot of the throne, and be trained to the work of intercession. Let us do so in the assurance that amidst our stammerings and fears He is carrying on His work most beautifully. He will breathe His own life, which is all prayer, into us. As He makes us partakers of His righteousness and His life, He will of His intercession too. As the members of His body, as a holy priesthood, we shall take part in His priestly work of pleading and prevailing with God for men. Yes, let us most joyfully say, ignorant and feeble though we be, 'Lord, teach us to pray.'

'Lord, Teach Us To Pray.'

Blessed Lord! who ever livest to pray, Thou canst teach me too to pray, me to live ever to pray. In [12]this Thou lovest to make me share Thy glory in heaven, that I should pray without ceasing, and ever stand as a priest in the presence of my God.

Lord Jesus! I ask Thee this day to enrol my name among those who confess that they know not how to pray as they ought, and especially ask Thee for a course of teaching in prayer. Lord! teach me to tarry with Thee in the school, and give Thee time to train me. May a deep sense of my ignorance, of the wonderful privilege and power of prayer, of the need of the Holy Spirit as the Spirit of prayer, lead me to cast away my thoughts of what I think I know, and make me kneel before Thee in true teachableness and poverty of spirit.

And fill me, Lord, with the confidence that with such a teacher as Thou art I shall learn to pray. In the assurance that I have as my teacher, Jesus, who is ever praying to the Father, and by His prayer rules the destinies of His Church and the world, I will not be afraid. As much as I need to know of the mysteries of the prayer-world, Thou wilt unfold for me. And when I may not know, Thou wilt teach me to be strong in faith, giving glory to

God.

Blessed Lord! Thou wilt not put to shame Thy scholar who trusts Thee, nor, by Thy grace, would he Thee either. Amen.

'IN SPIRIT AND TRUTH;'

OR

THE TRUE WORSHIPPERS.

'The hour cometh, and now is, when the true worshippers shall worship the Father in spirit and truth: for such doth the Father seek to be His worshippers. God is a Spirit: and they that worship Him must worship Him in spirit and truth.'—John iv. 23, 24.

These words of Jesus to the woman of Samaria are His first recorded teaching on the subject of prayer. They give us some wonderful first glimpses into the world of prayer. The Father seeks worshippers: our worship satisfies His loving heart and is a joy to Him. He seeks true worshippers, but finds many not such as He would have them. True worship is that which is in spirit and truth. The Son has come to open the way for this worship in spirit and in truth, and teach it us. And so one of our first lessons in the school of prayer must be to understand what it is to pray in spirit and in truth, and to know how we can attain to it.

[14]To the woman of Samaria our Lord spoke of a threefold worship. There is, first, the ignorant worship of the Samaritans: 'Ye worship that which ye know not.' The second, the intelligent worship of the Jew, having the true knowledge of God: 'We worship that which we know; for salvation is of the Jews.' And then the new, the spiritual worship which He Himself has come to introduce: 'The hour is coming, and is now, when the true worshippers shall worship the Father in spirit and truth.' From the connection it is evident that the words 'in spirit and truth' do not mean, as is often thought, earnestly, from the heart, in sincerity. The Samaritans had the five books of Moses and some knowledge of God; there was doubtless more than one among them who honestly and earnestly sought God in prayer. The Jews had the true full revelation of God in His word, as thus far given; there were among them godly men, who called upon God with their whole heart. And yet not 'in spirit and truth,' in the full meaning of the words. Jesus says, 'The hour is coming, and now is:' it is only in and through Him that the worship of God will be in spirit and truth.

Among Christians one still finds the three classes of worshippers. Some who in their ignorance hardly know what they ask: they pray earnestly, and yet receive but little. Others there are, who have more correct knowledge, who try to pray with all their [15]mind and heart, and often pray most earnestly, and yet do not attain to the full blessedness of worship in spirit and truth. It is into this third class we must ask our Lord Jesus to take us; we must be taught of Him how to worship in spirit and truth. This alone is spiritual worship; this makes us worshippers such as the Father seeks. In prayer everything will depend on our understanding well and practising the worship in spirit and truth.

'God is a Spirit and they that worship Him must worship Him in spirit and truth.' The first thought suggested here by the Master is that there must be harmony between God and His worshippers; such as God is, must His worship be. This is according to a principle which prevails throughout the universe: we look for correspondence between an object and the organ to which it reveals or yields itself. The eye has an inner fitness for the light, the ear for sound. The man who would truly worship God, would find and know and possess and enjoy God, must be in harmony with Him, must have a capacity for receiving Him. Because God is Spirit, we must worship in spirit. As God is, so His worshipper.

And what does this mean? The woman had asked our Lord whether Samaria or Jerusalem was the true place of worship. He answers that henceforth worship is no longer to be limited to a certain place: 'Woman, believe Me, the hour cometh when neither in [16]this mountain, nor in Jerusalem, shall ye worship the Father.' As God is Spirit, not bound by space or time, but in His infinite perfection always and everywhere the same, so His worship would henceforth no longer be confined by place or form, but spiritual as God Himself is spiritual. A lesson of deep importance. How much our Christianity suffers from this, that it is confined to certain times and places. A man who seeks to pray earnestly in the church or in the closet, spends the greater part of the week or the day in a spirit entirely at variance with that in which he prayed. His worship was the work of a fixed place or hour, not of his whole being. God is a spirit: He is the Everlasting and Unchangeable One; what He is, He is always and in truth. Our worship must even so be in spirit and truth: His worship must be the spirit of our life; our life must be worship in spirit as God is Spirit.

'God is a Spirit: and they that worship Him must worship Him in spirit and truth.' The second thought that comes to us is that this worship in the spirit must come from God Himself. God is Spirit: He alone has Spirit to give. It was for this He sent His Son, to fit us for such spiritual worship, by giving us the Holy Spirit. It is of His own work that Jesus speaks when He says twice, 'The hour cometh,' and then adds, 'and is now.' He came to baptize with the Holy Spirit; the Spirit could not stream [17]forth till He was glorified (John i. 33, vii. 37, 38, xvi. 7). It was when He had made an end of sin, and entering into the Holiest of all with His blood, had there on our behalf received the Holy Spirit (Acts ii. 33), that He could send Him down to us as the Spirit of the Father. It was when Christ had redeemed us, and we in Him had received the position of children, that the Father sent forth the Spirit of His Son into our hearts to cry, 'Abba, Father.' The worship in spirit is the worship of the Father in the Spirit of Christ, the Spirit of Sonship.

This is the reason why Jesus here uses the name of Father. We never find one of the Old Testament saints personally appropriate the name of child or call God his Father. The worship of the Father is only possible to those to whom the Spirit of the Son has been given. The worship in spirit is only possible to those to whom the Son has revealed the Father, and who have received the spirit of Sonship. It is only Christ who opens the way and teaches the worship in spirit.

And in truth. That does not only mean, in sincerity. Nor does it only signify, in accordance with the truth of God's Word. The expression is one of deep and Divine meaning. Jesus is 'the only-begotten of the Father, full of grace and truth.' 'The law was given by Moses; grace and truth came by Jesus Christ.' Jesus says, 'I am the truth and the life.' [18]In the Old Testament all was shadow and promise; Jesus brought and gives the reality, the substance, of things hoped for. In Him the blessings and powers of the eternal life are our actual possession and experience. Jesus is full of grace and truth; the Holy Spirit is the Spirit of truth; through Him the grace that is in Jesus is ours indeed, and truth a positive communication out of the Divine life. And so worship in spirit is worship in truth; actual living fellowship with God, a real correspondence and harmony between the Father, who is a Spirit, and the child praying in the spirit.

What Jesus said to the woman of Samaria, she could not at once understand. Pentecost was needed to reveal its full meaning. We are hardly prepared at our first entrance into the school of prayer to grasp such teaching. We shall understand it better later on. Let us only begin and take the lesson as He gives it. We are carnal and cannot bring God the worship He seeks. But Jesus came to give the Spirit: He has given Him to us. Let the disposition in which we set ourselves to pray be what Christ's words have taught us. Let there be the deep confession of our inability to bring God the worship that is pleasing to Him; the childlike teachableness that waits on Him to instruct us; the simple faith that yields itself to the breathing of the Spirit. Above all, let us hold fast the blessed truth—we shall find [19]that the Lord has more to say to us about it—that the knowledge of the Fatherhood of God, the revelation of His infinite Fatherliness in our hearts, the faith in the infinite love that gives us His Son and His Spirit to make us children, is indeed the secret of prayer in spirit and truth. This is the new and living way Christ opened up for us. To have Christ the Son, and The Spirit of the Son, dwelling within us, and revealing the Father, this makes us true, spiritual worshippers.

'Lord, Teach Us To Pray.'

Blessed Lord! I adore the love with which Thou didst teach a woman, who had refused Thee a cup of water, what the worship of God must be. I rejoice in the assurance that Thou wilt no less now instruct Thy disciple, who comes to Thee with a heart that longs to pray in spirit and in truth. O my Holy Master! do teach me this blessed secret.

Teach me that the worship in spirit and truth is not of man, but only comes from Thee; that it is not only a thing of times and seasons, but the outflowing of a life in Thee. Teach me to draw near to God in prayer under the deep impression of my ignorance and my having nothing in myself to offer Him, and at the same time of the provision Thou, my Saviour, makest for the Spirit's breathing in my [20]childlike stammerings. I do bless Thee that in Thee I am a child, and have a child's liberty of access; that in Thee I have the spirit of Sonship and of worship of truth. Teach me, above all, Blessed Son of the Father, how it is the revelation of the Father that gives confidence in prayer; and let the infinite Fatherliness of God's Heart be my joy and strength for a life of prayer and of worship. Amen.

[21]
PRAY TO THY FATHER WHICH IS IN SECRET

OR

ALONE WITH GOD.

'But thou, when thou prayest, enter into thine inner chamber, and having shut thy door, pray to thy Father which is in secret, and thy Father which seeth in secret shall recompense thee.'—Matt. vi. 6.

After Jesus had called His first disciples He gave them their first public teaching in the Sermon on the Mount. He there expounded to them the kingdom of God, its laws and its life. In that kingdom God is not only King, but Father; He not only gives all, but is Himself all. In the knowledge and fellowship of Him alone is its blessedness. Hence it came as a matter of course that the revelation of prayer and the prayer-life was a part of His teaching concerning the New Kingdom He came to set up. Moses gave neither command nor regulation with regard to prayer: even the prophets say little directly of the duty of prayer; it is Christ who teaches to pray.

[22]And the first thing the Lord teaches His disciples is that they must have a secret place for prayer; every one must have some solitary spot

18

where he can be alone with his God. Every teacher must have a schoolroom. We have learnt to know and accept Jesus as our only teacher in the school of prayer. He has already taught us at Samaria that worship is no longer confined to times and places; that worship, spiritual true worship, is a thing of the spirit and the life; the whole man must in his whole life be worship in spirit and truth. And yet He wants each one to choose for himself the fixed spot where He can daily meet him. That inner chamber, that solitary place, is Jesus' schoolroom. That spot may be anywhere; that spot may change from day to day if we have to change our abode; but that secret place there must be, with the quiet time in which the pupil places himself in the Master's presence, to be by Him prepared to worship the Father. There alone, but there most surely, Jesus comes to us to teach us to pray.

A teacher is always anxious that his schoolroom should be bright and attractive, filled with the light and air of heaven, a place where pupils long to come, and love to stay. In His first words on prayer in the Sermon on the Mount, Jesus seeks to set the inner chamber before us in its most attractive light. If we listen carefully, we soon notice what the chief [23]thing is He has to tell us of our tarrying there. Three times He uses the name of Father: 'Pray to thy Father;' 'Thy Father shall recompense thee;' Your Father knoweth what things ye have need of.' The first thing in closet-prayer is: I must meet my Father. The light that shines in the closet must be: the light of the Father's countenance. The fresh air from heaven with which Jesus would have filled the atmosphere in which I am to breathe and pray, is: God's Father-love, God's infinite Fatherliness. Thus each thought or petition we breathe out will be simple, hearty, childlike trust in the Father. This is how the Master teaches us to pray: He brings us into the Father's living presence. What we pray there must avail. Let us listen carefully to hear what the Lord has to say to us.

First, 'Pray to thy Father which is in secret.' God is a God who hides Himself to the carnal eye. As long as in our worship of God we are chiefly occupied with our own thoughts and exercises, we shall not meet Him who is a Spirit, the unseen One. But to the man who withdraws himself from all that is of the world and man, and prepares to wait upon God alone, the Father will reveal Himself. As he forsakes and gives up and shuts out the world, and the life of the world, and surrenders himself to be led of Christ into the secret of God's presence, the light of the Father's love will rise upon him. The secrecy of the inner [24]chamber and the closed door, the entire separation from all around us, is an image of, and so a help to, that inner spiritual sanctuary, the secret of God's tabernacle, within the veil, where our spirit truly comes into contact with the Invisible One. And so we are taught, at the very outset of our search after the secret of effectual prayer, to remember that it is in the inner chamber, where we are alone with the Father, that we shall learn to pray aright. The Father is in secret: in these words Jesus teaches us where He is waiting us, where He is always to be found. Christians often complain that private prayer is not what it should be. They feel weak and sinful, the heart is cold and dark; it is as if they have so little to pray, and in that little no faith or joy. They are discouraged and kept from prayer by the thought that they cannot come to the Father as they ought or as they wish. Child of God! listen to your Teacher. He tells you that when you go to private prayer your first thought must be: The Father is in secret, the Father waits me there. Just because your heart is cold and prayerless, get you into the presence of the loving Father. As a father pitieth his children, so the Lord pitieth you. Do not be thinking of how little you have to bring God, but of how much He wants to give you. Just place yourself before, and look up into, His face; think of His love, His wonderful, tender, pitying love. [25]Just tell Him how sinful and cold and dark all is: it is the Father's loving heart will give light and warmth to yours. O do what Jesus says: Just shut the door, and pray to thy Father, which is in secret. Is it not wonderful? to be able to go alone with God, the infinite God. And then to look up and say: My Father!

'And thy Father, which seeth in secret, will recompense thee.' Here Jesus assures us that secret prayer cannot be fruitless: its blessing will show itself in our life. We have but in secret, alone with God, to entrust our life before men to Him; He will reward us openly; He will see to it that the answer to prayer be made manifest in His blessing upon us. Our Lord would thus teach us that as infinite Fatherliness and Faithfulness is that with which God meets us in secret, so on our part there should be the childlike simplicity of faith, the confidence that our prayer does bring down a blessing. 'He that cometh to God must believe that He is a rewarder of them that seek Him.' Not on the strong or the fervent feeling with which I pray does the blessing of the closet depend, but upon the love and the power of the Father to whom I there entrust my needs. And therefore the Master has but one desire: Remember your Father is, and sees and hears in secret; go there and stay there, and go again from there in the confidence: He will recompense. Trust Him for it; [26]depend upon Him: prayer to the Father cannot be vain; He will reward you openly.

Still further to confirm this faith in the Father-love of God, Christ speaks a third word: 'Your Father knoweth what things ye have need of before ye ask Him.' At first sight it might appear as if this thought made prayer less needful: God knows far better than we what we need. But as we get a deeper insight into what prayer really is, this truth will help much to strengthen our faith. It will teach us that we do not need, as the heathen, with the multitude and urgency of our words, to compel an unwilling God to listen to us. It will lead to a holy thoughtfulness and silence in prayer as it suggests the question: Does my Father really know that I need this? It will, when once we have been led by the Spirit to the certainty that our request is indeed something that, according to the Word, we do need for God's glory, give us wonderful confidence to say, My Father knows I need it and must have it. And if there be any delay in the answer, it will teach us in quiet perseverance to hold on: Father! Thou knowest I need it. O the blessed liberty and simplicity of a child that Christ our Teacher would fain cultivate in us, as we draw near to God: let us look up to the Father until His Spirit works it in us. Let us sometimes in our prayers, when we are in danger of being so occupied with our fervent, urgent [27]petitions, as to forget that the Father knows and hears, let us hold still and just quietly say: My Father sees, my Father hears, my Father knows; it will help our faith to take the answer, and to say: We know that we have the petitions we have asked of Him.

And now, all ye who have anew entered the school of Christ to be taught to pray, take these lessons, practise them, and trust Him to perfect you in them. Dwell much in the inner chamber, with the door shut—shut in from men, shut up with God; it is there the Father waits you, it is there Jesus will teach you to pray. To be alone in secret with the Father: this be your highest joy. To be assured that the Father will openly reward the secret prayer, so that it cannot remain unblessed: this be your strength day by day. And to know that the Father knows that you need what you ask, this be your liberty to bring every need, in the assurance that your God will supply it according to His riches in glory in Christ Jesus.

'Lord, teach us to pray.'

Blessed Saviour! with my whole heart I do bless Thee for the appointment of the inner chamber, as the school where Thou meetest each of Thy pupils alone, and revealest to him the Father. O my Lord! strengthen my faith so in the Father's tender love and kindness, that as often as I feel sinful or [28]troubled, the first instinctive thought may be to go where I know the Father waits me, and where prayer never can go unblessed. Let the thought that He knows my need before I ask, bring me, in great restfulness of faith, to trust that He will give what His child requires. O let the place of secret prayer become to me the most beloved spot on earth.

And, Lord! hear me as I pray that Thou wouldest everywhere bless the closets of Thy believing people. Let Thy wonderful revelation of a Father's tenderness free all young Christians from every thought of secret prayer as a duty or a burden, and lead them to regard it as the highest privilege of their life, a joy and a blessing. Bring back all who are discouraged, because they cannot find aught to bring Thee in prayer. O give them to understand that they have only to come with their emptiness to Him who has all to give, and delights to do it. Not, what they have to bring the Father, but what the Father waits to give them, be their one thought.

And bless especially the inner chamber of all Thy servants who are working for Thee, as the place where God's truth and God's grace is revealed to them, where they are daily anointed with fresh oil, where their strength is renewed, and the blessings are received in faith, with which they are to bless their fellow-men. Lord, draw us all in the closet nearer to Thyself and the Father. Amen.

[29]
'AFTER THIS MANNER PRAY;'

OR

THE MODEL PRAYER.

'After this manner therefore pray ye: Our Father which art in heaven.'—
Matt. vi. 9.

Every teacher knows the power of example. He not only tells the child what to do and how to do it, but shows him how it really can be done. In condescension to our weakness, our Heavenly Teacher has given us the very words we are to take with us as we draw near to our Father. We have in them a form of prayer in which there breathe the freshness and fulness of the Eternal Life. So simple that the child can lisp it, so divinely rich that it comprehends all that God can give. A form of prayer that becomes the model and inspiration for all other prayer, and yet always draws us back to itself as the deepest utterance of our souls before our God.

'Our Father which art in heaven!' To appreciate this word of adoration aright, I must remember that [30]none of the saints had in Scripture ever ventured to address God as their Father. The invocation places us at once in the centre of the wonderful revelation the Son came to make of His Father as our Father too. It comprehends the mystery of redemption— Christ delivering us from the curse that we might become the children of God. The mystery of regeneration—the Spirit in the new birth giving us the new life. And the mystery of faith—ere yet the redemption is accomplished or understood, the word is given on the lips of the disciples to prepare them for the blessed experience still to come. The words are the key to the whole prayer, to all prayer. It takes time, it takes life to study them; it will take eternity to understand them fully. The knowledge of God's Father-love is the first and simplest, but also the last and highest lesson in the school of prayer. It is in the personal relation to the living God, and the personal conscious fellowship of love with Himself, that prayer begins. It is in the knowledge of God's Fatherliness, revealed by the Holy Spirit, that the power of prayer will be found to root and grow. In the infinite tenderness

23

and pity and patience of the infinite Father, in His loving readiness to hear and to help, the life of prayer has its joy. O let us take time, until the Spirit has made these words to us spirit and truth, filling heart and life: 'Our Father which art in heaven.' Then we are indeed within [31]the veil, in the secret place of power where prayer always prevails.

'Hallowed be Thy name.' There is something here that strikes us at once.

24

While we ordinarily first bring our own needs to God in prayer, and then think of what belongs to God and His interests, the Master reverses the order. First, Thy name, Thy kingdom, Thy will; then, give us, forgive us, lead us, deliver us. The lesson is of more importance than we think. In true worship the Father must be first, must be all. The sooner I learn to forget myself in the desire that He may be glorified, the richer will the blessing be that prayer will bring to myself. No one ever loses by what he sacrifices for the Father.

This must influence all our prayer. There are two sorts of prayer: personal and intercessory. The latter ordinarily occupies the lesser part of our time and energy. This may not be. Christ has opened the school of prayer specially to train intercessors for the great work of bringing down, by their faith and prayer, the blessings of His work and love on the world around. There can be no deep growth in prayer unless this be made our aim. The little child may ask of the father only what it needs for itself; and yet it soon learns to say, Give some for sister too. But the grown-up son, who only lives for the father's interest and takes charge of the father's business, asks more largely, and gets all that is asked. And [32]Jesus would train us to the blessed life of consecration and service, in which our interests are all subordinate to the Name, and the Kingdom, and the Will of the Father. O let us live for this, and let, on each act of adoration, Our Father! there follow in the same breath, Thy Name, Thy Kingdom, Thy Will;—for this we look up and long.

25

'Hallowed be Thy name..' What name? This new name of Father. The word Holy is the central word of the Old Testament; the name Father of the New. In this name of Love all the holiness and glory of God are now to be revealed. And how is the name to be hallowed? By God Himself: 'I will hallow My great name which ye have profaned.' Our prayer must be that in ourselves, in all God's children, in presence of the world, God Himself would reveal the holiness, the Divine power, the hidden glory of the name of Father. The Spirit of the Father is the Holy Spirit: it is only when we yield ourselves to be led of Him, that the name will be hallowed in our prayer and our lives. Let us learn the prayer: 'Our Father, hallowed be Thy name.'

'Thy kingdom come.' The Father is a King and has a kingdom. The son and heir of a king has no higher ambition than the glory of his father's kingdom. In time of war or danger this becomes his passion; he can think of nothing else. The children of the Father are here in the enemy's territory, where [33]the kingdom, which is in heaven, is not yet fully manifested. What more natural than that, when they learn to hallow the Father-name, they should long and cry with deep enthusiasm: 'Thy kingdom come.' The coming of the kingdom is the one great event on which the revelation of the Father's glory, the blessedness of His children, the salvation of the world depends. On our prayers too the coming of the kingdom waits. Shall we not join in the deep longing cry of the redeemed: 'Thy kingdom come'? Let us learn it in the school of Jesus.

'Thy will be done, as in heaven, so on earth.' This petition is too frequently applied alone to the suffering of the will of God. In heaven God's will is done, and the Master teaches the child to ask that the will may be done on earth just as in heaven: in the spirit of adoring submission and ready obedience. Because the will of God is the glory of heaven, the doing of it is the blessedness of heaven. As the will is done, the kingdom of heaven

27

comes into the heart. And wherever faith has accepted the Father's love, obedience accepts the Father's will. The surrender to, and the prayer for a life of heaven-like obedience, is the spirit of childlike prayer.

'Give us this day our daily bread.' When first the child has yielded himself to the Father in the care for His Name, His Kingdom, and His Will, he has full liberty to ask for his daily bread. A master [34]cares for the food of his servant, a general of his soldiers, a father of his child. And will not the Father in heaven care for the child who has in prayer given himself up to His interests? We may indeed in full confidence say: Father, I live for Thy honor and Thy work; I know Thou carest for me. Consecration to God and His will gives wonderful liberty in prayer for temporal things: the whole earthly life is given to the Father's loving care.

'And forgive us our debts as we also have forgiven our debtors.' As bread is the first need of the body, so forgiveness for the soul. And the provision for the one is as sure as for the other. We are children, but sinners too; our right of access to the Father's presence we owe to the precious blood and the forgiveness it has won for us. Let us beware of the prayer for forgiveness becoming a formality: only what is really confessed is really forgiven. Let us in faith accept the forgiveness as promised: as a spiritual reality, an actual transaction between God and us, it is the entrance into all the Father's love and all the privileges of children. Such forgiveness, as a living experience, is impossible without a forgiving spirit to others: as forgiven expresses the heavenward, so forgiving the earthward, relation of God's child. In each prayer to the Father I must be able to say that I know of no one whom I do not heartily love.

'And lead us not into temptation, but deliver us [35]from the evil one.' Our daily bread, the pardon of our sins, and then our being kept from all sin and the power of the evil one, in these three petitions all our personal need is comprehended. The prayer for bread and pardon must be accompanied by the surrender to live in all things in holy obedience to the Father's will, and the believing prayer in everything to be kept by the power of the indwelling Spirit from the power of the evil one.

Children of God! it is thus Jesus would have us to pray to the Father in heaven. O let His Name, and Kingdom, and Will, have the first place in our love; His providing, and pardoning, and keeping love will be our sure

31

portion. So the prayer will lead us up to the true child-life: the Father all to the child, the Father all for the child. We shall understand how Father and child, the Thine and the Our, are all one, and how the heart that begins its prayer with the God-devoted Thine, will have the power in faith to speak out the Our too. Such prayer will, indeed, be the fellowship and interchange of love, always bringing us back in trust and worship to Him who is not only the Beginning but the End: 'For thine is the kingdom, and the power, and the glory, for ever, Amen.' Son of the Father, teach us to pray, 'Our Father.'

'Lord, teach us to pray.'

[36]O Thou who art the only-begotten Son, teach us, we beseech Thee, to pray, 'Our Father.' We thank Thee, Lord, for these Living Blessed Words which Thou hast given us. We thank Thee for the millions who in them have learnt to know and worship the Father, and for what they have been to us. Lord! it is as if we needed days and weeks in Thy school with each separate petition; so deep and full are they. But we look to Thee to lead us deeper into their meaning: do it, we pray Thee, for Thy Name's sake; Thy name is Son of the Father.

Lord! Thou didst once say: 'No man knoweth the Father save the Son, and he to whom the Son willeth to reveal Him.' And again: 'I made known unto them Thy name, and will make it known, that the love wherewith Thou hast loved Me may be in them.' Lord Jesus! reveal to us the Father. Let His name, His infinite Father-love, the love with which He loved Thee, according to Thy prayer, BE IN US. Then shall we say aright, 'Our Father!' Then shall we apprehend Thy teaching, and the first spontaneous breathing of our heart will be: 'Our Father, Thy Name, Thy Kingdom, Thy Will.' And we shall bring our needs and our sins and our temptations to Him in the confidence that the love of such a Father cares for all.

Blessed Lord! we are Thy scholars, we trust Thee; do teach us to pray, 'Our Father.' Amen.

Disclaimer and Terms of Use: The Author and Publisher have strived to be as accurate and complete as possible in the creation of this book, notwithstanding the fact that he does not warrant or represent at any time that the contents within are accurate due to the rapidly changing nature of the Internet. While all attempts have been made to verify information provided in this publication, the Author and Publisher assume no responsibility for errors, omissions, or contrary interpretation of the subject matter herein. Any perceived slights of specific persons, people, or organizations are unintentional. In practical advice books, like anything else in life, there are no guarantees of results. Readers are cautioned to rely on their own judgment about their individual circumstances and act accordingly. This book is not intended for use as a source of legal, medical, business, accounting or financial advice. All readers are advised to seek the services of competent professionals in the legal, medical, business, accounting, and finance fields.

Made in the USA
Monee, IL
25 April 2021

66860669R00020